# AMANI

## (of The Black Space Plays)

by a.k. payne

# ‖SAMUEL FRENCH‖

No one shall make any changes in this title(s) for the purpose of production. No part of this book may be reproduced, stored in a retrieval system, scanned, uploaded, or transmitted in any form, by any means, now known or yet to be invented, including mechanical, electronic, digital, photocopying, recording, videotaping, or otherwise, without the prior written permission of the publisher. No one shall share this title(s), or any part of this title(s), through any social media or file hosting websites.

For all inquiries regarding motion picture, television, online/digital and other media rights, please contact Concord Theatricals Corp.

## MUSIC AND THIRD-PARTY MATERIALS USE NOTE

Licensees are solely responsible for obtaining formal written permission from copyright owners to use copyrighted music and/or other copyrighted third-party materials (e.g. artworks, logos) in the performance of this play and are strongly cautioned to do so. If no such permission is obtained by the licensee, then the licensee must use only original music and materials that the licensee owns and controls. Licensees are solely responsible and liable for clearances of all third-party copyrighted materials, including without limitation music, and shall indemnify the copyright owners of the play(s) and their licensing agent, Concord Theatricals Corp., against any costs, expenses, losses and liabilities arising from the use of such copyrighted third-party materials by licensees. For music, please contact the appropriate music licensing authority in your territory for the rights to any incidental music.

## IMPORTANT BILLING AND CREDIT REQUIREMENTS

If you have obtained performance rights to this title, please refer to your licensing agreement for important billing and credit requirements.

*AMANI* was first co-produced by National Black Theatre (Sade Lythcott, Executive Artistic Director; Jonathan McCrory, Executive Artistic Director) and Rattlestick Theater (Daniella Topol, Artistic Director) and premiered at Rattlestick Theater in New York City on February 8, 2023. The production was directed by Josiah Davis, with set design by Maruti Evans, costume design by Mika Eubanks, sound design and original music by Kathy Ruvuna, lighting design by Marika Kent, projection design by Brittany Bland, and dramaturgy by Nissy Aya. The production stage manager was Kiara Brown. The cast was as follows:

**SMITH** . . . . . . . . . . . . . . . . . . . . . . . . . . . . . . . . . . . . . . Eden Marryshow

**AMANI** . . . . . . . . . . . . . . . . . . . . . . . . . . . . . . . . . . . . . Denise Manning

**KOFA** . . . . . . . . . . . . . . . . . . . . . . . . . . . . . . . . . . . . . . . . . Kai Heath

**DASIA** . . . . . . . . . . . . . . . . . . . . . . . . . . . . . . . . . . . . . . Mars Rucker

**ROBERT RICHARDS / DAVION / LAMAR DAVIS /**
   **A SERIES OF MEN (ASOM...)** . . . . . . . . . . . . . Omari  K. Chancellor

# PLAYWRIGHT'S NOTES

unless the script says otherwise or the choice is intentional, words should read like they are your auntie talking shit in your living room. if that is not a reference that is yours, actors should resist the urge to "perform" poetry or to amplify the text's heightened language beyond itself. characters should be as they be: our everyday tongue is full of poems. there is a tendency to weigh "lyrical/poetic" plays about Black people down with melancholy and render them slow and sacred in moments where they have not asked to be slow nor sacred. allow the moments of rest and quiet in this play to HAPPEN where they happen... and they happen. i am not interested here in English as sacred or right; i am interested in what we do and how we speak as it fails. our lives are not tragedies: whoever directs this must know what it means to hold both joy and pain at once, i.e. the essence of the Blues.

**Brief Guide on Slashes**

- mid-line (ML) slash: actor interrupted or conjoined in text /"here"; proceed through the line

- beginning of the line (BL) slash: the line thereafter is an interruption; begin this interruption at the preceding ML slash

- continuous BL slashes: there is a rhythm/somewhat percussive tempo for which all actors in a section of text are responsible, limit air between lines, a cascade or wave

*for Blackgirl me of yesterday*

# COMMUNITY

### (everybody is Black)

**SMITH** – Amani's father, he/him, 1970–2021

**AMANI** – a Blackgirl becoming grown perhaps dreaming towards more true language, she/her/many, 1995–; *[this actor may identify as nonbinary and/or as a Blackwoman; this actor also may just be themself i.e. this actor may refuse to subscribe to any label bout they body and instead may simply wish to breathe with the deep awareness of gender as an infinite spectrum & English as this Black Atlantic tongue's first prison]

**KOFA** – Amani's first love & first friend, an astrophysicist and only child, (m)any pronouns, a gender-expansive person and/or a Black lesbian defying gender binaries

**DASIA** – a spirit, a narrator, Amani's mother, she/they, 1972–1997; *see bracketed note above

**ROBERT RICHARDS / DAVION / LAMAR DAVIS /
A SERIES OF MEN (ASOM…)** – an actor who plays a Man

# NOTE ON MUSIC

There is a song sung repeatedly in this play: Abbey Lincoln's 1959 rendition of "Afro Blue." Permission to perform the song in performances of *AMANI* is included in a production license, however, this does not include permission to exhibit any recordings of "Afro Blue."

## SETTING

*it's summer* [1]
*in this city*
*so at night, down the hill*
*gunshots pop*
*and in the morning*
*there a new name to remember*
*lest we forget*

*and*

*the street and this yard always*
*smell like barbecue*
*or lingering barbecue*


## TIME

*so days are forever*
*and nights are forever*

*and we know we are beautiful*
*and ugly too*

*the first quarter of the twenty-first century*
*rears her head in a series of dreams and*
*memories*

*somebody's mowing they lawn*
*too early in the morning*

*and everybody is sweating*

---

[1] italicized text may be performed by **DASIA** according to the director/
ensemble's discretion; if they are unspoken, make the play's world sing
them

**1**

## the beginning, a return

*in the garden, at a changing time: a dusk or
dawn*
**AMANI** *plays a hand game with* **KOFA**,
*a childhood friend*

*eventually they lower their hands
and just face one another
full of breath*

*we see this first
an instant
and then it is gone
like a blink*

*before*

**SMITH**, *a soft man bout his ways
stumbles through
front gate of a great yellow house
before which be
a garden dead
or in a space before and after living*

*he dons orange jumpsuit
drags garbage bag full of things
hasn't been here in six years.*

*the street*
*he walked down*
*to arrive here*
*is one he is trying*
*to search his memory for:*

*there is a store that was not there then*
*a person*
*who waved to him*
*who he cannot remember*

*did we love each other once?*
*did we share a joke in class?*

*he enters this gate*
*he stares at this house*
*looming testament*
*of dreams deferred*

*all this*
*takes all the time*
*it so requires*

*and when the time say so*

**SMITH** *falls to his knees*
*crumbles*
*and weeps;*
*his tears*
*draw*
*forth*
*memory*

*a glass cage appears*

*in four parts*
*from the wings*

*a prison*
*visiting room*

*it closes in on him*
*till there is no breath*
*to be breathed in this garden*

*he tries to fight against it*
*but he can't fight against it*

*it is coming for him*
*like it is coming for you*

*it must be clear*
*that it is also coming*
*for you*

*he screams*
*thrashes*
*screams again*

*there is no escape*

*and then a memory comes rushing*
*from the wings*

*a grounding*
*a reason:*

**AMANI**
*she is nine.*

> **SMITH** *and* **AMANI** *stare at each other*
> *through the glass*
> *for a long time—*
> *breath*
> *and breath*
> *and breath*
>
> *in which* **SMITH** *can settle*
>
> *and then they together*
> *pick up a phone*
> *and*
> *GO*

**AMANI.**  robert richards said
i'm too short to play basketball
even though i make more free throws than him

**SMITH.**  you tell him to shut up?

**AMANI.**  course i did.
then he said

> **ROBERT RICHARDS** *appears*
> *at the edge of the garden*

**ROBERT RICHARDS.**  you should just stay off the
court
you messing up the whole game tryna play.
you not even cute.
you should stop tryna be cute
before you fall and hurt yourself

**AMANI.**  and i said he'sstupid. and he's just mad
cause i make him look like he got no game

i said my dad taught me how to play
good as Jordan
or Lebron
since i was three
so i'm the best.

**SMITH.**  that's right

**AMANI.**  the greatest of all time.

**SMITH.**  that's right

**ROBERT RICHARDS.**  nobody
even watches the WNBA

**AMANI.**  when i get on there
they gonna watch the WNBA
just you wait and see
i *might* play you out of the NBA
i might be the first girl in the N-B-A
cause i'm that good
dribbling circles around you
cause i'm *that good.*

**ROBERT RICHARDS.**  shutupyounotevencute

**AMANI.**  who was even talking
about being cute

**ROBERT RICHARDS.**  that's all girls care about
being cute
and tryna show off for boys

**AMANI.**  ain't nobody talking about you
i'm talking about me

**ROBERT RICHARDS.**  whut

**AMANI.**  i said. i'm talking. about ME.

**ROBERT RICHARDS.**  let me kiss you

**AMANI.**  ew gross!

 and i was just real confused
 at that point
 cause i didn't really understand
 what kissing and being cute
 had to do with
 me making more free throws than him
 and me being in the WNBA.
 but robert richards is twelve
 and he thinks he knows everything
 even though i told him
 that twelve is not even all that old
 i'll be twelve in no time at all
 by the time i'm twelve
 my dad'll be here
 so i know it's no time at all.

 and he shrugged his shoulders
 and went down the street
 to get some nowlaters
 and he got me a pack
 even though i didn't ask for none
 and i don't even like nowlaters all like that
 especially not from that cornerstore
 cause they always hard
 and from like 1987

 **SMITH** *laughs, joy's reprieve*

and the lady always look at us
like we ugly and drops the change in our hands
from way up high.

but i took the nowlaters anyway
and i ate one
and it was so hard that by the time it was gone
the sun was setting
and the streetlights were coming on
and nana was telling me
i had to come in the house
and the fireflies were coming out
and robert richards was grabbing my hand

**ROBERT RICHARDS.** stay for five more minutes
let me catch a firefly for you

**AMANI.** boy get offa my hand

**ROBERT RICHARDS.** why you gotta be so
stuck up

**AMANI.** i'm not even stuck up
your hand just sweaty &
it's too hot to be holding hands.
wait till the trees turn orange
and i'll think about it.

**ROBERT RICHARDS.** by the time the trees turn
orange
i'mma find some other
girl to hold my hand

**AMANI.** and i was like...aight.
and he sucked his teeth like...

**ROBERT RICHARDS**. psh whatever
    i don't even like you
    anyway
    give me back
    my nowlaters then

**AMANI**. and i was like fine BYE
    cause by that time nana
    was holding the screen door open
    and screaming and if nana
    holds the screen door open
    for too long and the flies get in
    i wouldn't hear the end of that.

    plusssss i ain't even ask for his
    crusty nowlaters anyway.

        **SMITH** *laughs; a beat*

        **ROBERT RICHARDS** *leaves the garden*

is it cold in there?

**SMITH**. they got the air on blast
    feel like it's forever winter

**AMANI**. you got blankets?

**SMITH**. how is school?

**AMANI**. take your father to school day was stupid.
    raven kept bragging about how her daddy
    had a bmw and was bringing her lunch from
    burger king
    until jaylen was like burger king fries
    are soggy anyway and my daddy got a mercedes

and they kept arguing and arguing
until recess when all the fathers came
and we all saw that both their daddys
just had regular cars
w dents in the back
and ms. jacobs kept trying
to tell me it's okay
that i don't have a dad

and i said to her: "i have a dad"
but she *kept* looking at me
like she felt sorry for me
all the way until the final bell
and even the next morning

and i started thinking
maybe i hadn't said anything at all
like maybe i just said "i have a dad" in my head

i be thinking maybe i say lots of stuff just in my
head
like maybe when i speak it just sound like air
and maybe...
i don't know...

**SMITH.** what?

**AMANI.** like if only i know it
and no one else know it
and no one else can see or feel it
is it true? can it be real or possible?

like if i'm the only one who's seen you
and to all the world you ghost
do i have a dad?

SMITH.  of course.

>   and you are possible.
>   everything you know
>   and feel
>   is real.
>
>   and i ain't nobody's ghost
>   nobody tryna make me ghost
>   will succeed in taking away your dad

>       *beat*

AMANI.  you got a window

>   in your room?
>   can you see the sky?
>   it's real blue today.
>
>   i took a picture of it right before i came in
>   but the security guard
>   told nana i couldn't
>   bring it in to show you
>
>   she started yelling at him
>   she's probably still yelling at him

SMITH.  windows are dusty
>   i can imagine it though

AMANI.  when you imagine it what it look like?
>   it the bluest blue?

SMITH.  a couple clouds.

AMANI.  there's no clouds today
>   it's bluer than i've ever seen it

*beat*

dad
my mama
loved studying the stars?

**SMITH.**  could name every constellation

**AMANI & SMITH.**  andromeda
antlia
apus
aquarius
aquila
ara
aries

**SMITH.**  could locate venus
with a naked eye

in another life
maybe was an astronaut

**AMANI.**  you got a
beard now

**SMITH.**  *(laughing)* i know

**AMANI.**  you gonna
shave that off?
you look like
santa claus

**SMITH.**  *(laughing)* hey!

**AMANI.**  i'm juuuuust saying

**SMITH**.  costs five ramen noodles
for a haircut
i'm saving up

**AMANI**.  *(laughing)* okay
ya need to handle that.
you think they'd
let me bring you ramen noodles?

**SMITH**.  nah.

nothing goes in or out.

**AMANI**.  what's it smell like?

**SMITH**.  how is nana?

**AMANI**.  her feet always hurting.
cousin laylee pregnant again
and nana say she ain't helping her raise this one
her feet hurt too much, she says
she keeps asking me about blood
like if i've seen blood
and i don't know what she's talking about
she keeps saying
i need to tell her
soon as i see some blood

i think she's okay
except for her feet always hurting
i think she's okay.

> *beat*

dad?

**SMITH**.  unhuhh

**AMANI.** have ya made friends?

> **SMITH** *chuckles at this question's*
> *allusion to a simpler world*
> *than the one in which he finds himself*

**SMITH.** yeah lotsa dudes from the block are in here.

people who disappeared
people you forgot disappeared

this one dude i used to throw
dice with in the bathroom
in high school
used to fight
everybody over everything.
he got shot
and in a wheelchair—
now in here.

dude who used to tell
jokes in class all the time
even though nobody
thought he was funny

we all in here
we've aged a lot though
not from time

we look like high school
was millennia
ago

**AMANI.** it sounds like a family
reunion like the ones
we have in the park?

> *beat*
>
> **SMITH** *tries his best to breathe in the deep sadness*
>
> *of the distance between his daughter and himself*
>
> *he finds he can only laugh at first in the light behind his daughter's eyes*
>
> *he finds he can no longer pivot; he tries to never lie*

**SMITH.** nah, mani.

they make us remember
all the time
that we are not boys anymore

we are not even

men

anymore.

there's a whole lot of silence
and a whole lot of sizing each other up in that silence
and no too sweet cherry cool-aid
and no aunt j talking shit on everybody
and no pool to jump in when it gets too hot
which ain't really a reunion at all
actually

everybody
is trying to find in
the next person's eyes
what happened
and how they got us too

and how we supposed to get out of here
and why everything feels so
endless, so absolute. so goddamn slow

we try to forget
that we got to sleep
when the sun goes down
like we are ten again
and there is no difference
between day and night
cause the windows
are so dusty
and we got to piss in pots
once the cells are closed
and we got to talk to our daughters
through glass
and we try to remember
try to find little bits of things
to remind us we are human.
and
i
i
um
i
i
hey
i'm sorry
i

> **SMITH** *is crying.* **AMANI** *is not;*
> *it should be strange that* **AMANI** *is not*

**AMANI**.  it's okay dad.

> *something indicates their time is up.*
> *no voices of guards or no shit like that.*
> *this ain't their play.*

**SMITH**.  i love you

**AMANI**.  i love you too.
try to see me through the window?
i'll be waving.

**SMITH**.  i'll try.
i'll wave too.
tell nana to stop arguing
with them niggas.
that ain't her fight
tell her to get some good shoes
for her feet.

**AMANI**.  okay

**SMITH**.  what i tell you?

**AMANI**.  we come from light and we still light

**SMITH**.  and where the light shine

**AMANI**.  wherever we go.

> *and then the cage*
> *releases at once*
> *and* **SMITH**
> *collapses*
> *in that same garden*
> *out of breath*

*is he free yet?*
*are we free yet?*

*he tears off the suit*
*until he is standing*
*in just underwear*
*and his body*
*in all of this, the garden grows*
*and grows*
*and grows*

*and so enters*
*the ghost of* **DASIA**

*they stare at each other*
**SMITH**
*slows his breath*
*this all takes a very*
*long time*

*this is how long*
*it takes to even start healing*
*to even remember*
*we can breathe.*

*make motherfuckers*
*wait.*

## 2

## 2007

*then, just before dawn*
*they sing*

**DASIA.**  dream of a land
my soul is from
i hear a hand
stroke on a drum

*throughout this*
***SMITH*** *reclothes himself*
*in a pair of jeans*
*a flannel shirt*
*boots and baseball cap*
***DASIA*** *and* ***SMITH***
*clean the yard and stage*
*and carry on two by fours,*
*buckets of paint*
*an assortment of hand tools,*
*the haphazard beginnings of what will come*
*to be the rocketship*
***SMITH*** *and* ***DASIA*** *get to work*
*there is a rhythm*
*in this work before the sun*

**SMITH.**  elegant boy
beautiful girl
dancing for joy
delicate whirl

**DASIA.**  two young lovers
    face to face
    with undulating grace
    they gently sway
    then slip away
    to some secluded place

**SMITH.**  whispering trees
    echo their sighs
    passionate pleas
    tender replies

    lovers in flight
    upward they glide
    burst at the height
    slowly subside

**DASIA.**  and my slumbering fantasy
    assumes reality
    until it seems it's not a dream

**SMITH.**  until it seems it's not a dream

**DASIA.**  until it seems it's not a dream

**SMITH & DASIA.**  for two for you and me

    **DASIA** *crosses beyond the garden*

    **SMITH** *grieves*
    *this departure*
    *each morning*

    *he finds a notice that has landed in the weeds*

**SMITH.**  *(a whisper)* shades of delight
    cocoa hue

rich as the night

afro blue

> *he reads the notice, FORECLOSURE*
> *crumples it*
> *pulls out a flask*
> *and takes a swig*
>
> *and so up comes the sun*

mani!

this garden won't wait for you!

things die while you sleep past the sun!

> *from the second floor window*
> *which is open cause it's hot*

**AMANI.** it's sunday! the sun's day! sun say i can sleep!

**SMITH.** and i say get up!

and i gave you life!

so i got as much say as the sun!

> **SMITH** *keeps working.*
> *eventually* **AMANI** *enters*
>
> *allow everything in this play to take as long*
> *as it takes*
>
> **AMANI** *is twelve now.*
> *she drags the hose from the backyard*
> *eyeing her father*
> *like 'it's literally six a.m.'*
> *he eyes her back*
> *like 'you got something to say?'*
> *she begins watering her garden*

**AMANI.**  ms. davidson said physics won't let something heavy like wood fly.

**SMITH.**  ms. davidson don't know nothing about your father.

**AMANI.**  i wrote a note to kofa

said

my father building a rocketship
and goin
to outer space
kofa wrote back in the corner

> **KOFA** *emerges at the edge of the garden*

**KOFA.**  'i believe it
which planet'

**AMANI.**  *(as **KOFA** draws across the sky)*
and drew all eight plus
pluto cross the top
complete
wit all the moons

> **KOFA** *exits the garden*

this was sposed to be language arts
not science
plus right now in science we learnin
bout the velocities
of rollercoasters

so

i ain't get to respond
'fore ms. davidson
snatched the letter off kofa's desk

and looked at me
like i was stupid

she threatened to give us detention
for making up lies

even though i told her it wasn't a lie
and you were really forreal making a rocketship
and gonna go to the moon

**SMITH.**  ms. davidson don't know nothing. think she so
smart cause she went to college.
fuck all that. i can build a house from the ground up
with just my two hands
bet i can build a ship.
the earth is wood
and wood the earth
if i can't fly with stuff of this earth
what gon give me wings?
if i don't love nothin in this world
i love this earth

**AMANI.**  and me.

**SMITH.**  course you.

    *beat*

**AMANI.**  what's that word mean?
the one that keeps showing up outside the house
FORECLOSURE.

**SMITH.**  measure this here.

**AMANI.**  daaaaad it's so earlyyyyy.

**SMITH.**  measure. this. here.

**AMANI.**  ughhhhh

two feet and...how many dots are in a foot?

**SMITH.** inches they called inches. twelve.

you know this, amani.

**AMANI.** why we don't use the other side of the tape. with
the centime—

**SMITH.** we just don't.

**AMANI.** y not?

**SMITH.** cause it ain't the way.

**AMANI.** who say?

**SMITH.** the man.

**AMANI.** who the man?

**SMITH.** he who writes my checks.

**AMANI.** but here nobody write your checks.

**SMITH.** still we got to be like the Man. cause he rule the
world.
until you take over. until you rule the world
we got to be like the Man.
that's why i work much as i do
that's why i learned a trade
that's why this your house.
so you can have some space.
so one day you can rule the world.
so one day we don't have to be like the Man.

**AMANI.** what if i don't want to rule the world
what if i just want to be in it?

**SMITH.** there's the rulers
and the ruled
that's how it go.

    sun rising
    come on now

**AMANI.**  two feet and twenty-six inches.

**SMITH.**  break those inches into feet

    I told you twelve inches in a foot so...

**AMANI.**  four feet and two inches.

**SMITH.**  good.
    amani you got to pay attention
    you got to take your time
    you in the seventh grade
    you're smart
    you know your numbers

**AMANI.**  i *know* i'm smart
    there's just
    there's all these rules
    some random somebody made
    bout numbers
    don't get why i got to follow them
    don't get what they got to do w me

    i like reading.
    i'm good at reading.

**SMITH.**  you can't just be good at one thing
    world like this

    you got to be good at everything

    and cut this. here real careful. watch me now.
    watch me. when you wanna make a cut you make a
    crow's foot like this—

**AMANI**.  look like a check mark

**SMITH**.  unhuhh… but you make that mark and that's
where your knife
gonna go right into the crevice, see and you cut there
and then you snap
like that. i'mma stand right here so you don't cut
something that don't need to be cut.
alright now, go head

> **AMANI** *snaps the wood*

good.

> **AMANI** *goes back to watering her garden*

**AMANI**.  dad
you say my mama
loved studying the stars?

**SMITH**.  yeah
could name every constellation

**DASIA**.  andromeda
antlia
apus
aquarius
aquila
ara
aries…

**AMANI**.  could locate venus
with a naked eye

i think
i had a dream about her.

**SMITH**.  mani it's too early.

**AMANI**. and yet here i am
  awake

**SMITH**. amani —

  why you always wanna talk about her
  when it's too early in the morning?

**AMANI**. cause i dream at night
  and she come at night
  when i dream

      *beat*

  dad

**SMITH**. what mani?

**AMANI**. i won't ask again.

**SMITH**. you say that every time you ask

  you look like her
  you talk like her
  your eyes the same color
  you got the same hair
  thick as this garden
  which she loved to grow
  which why you got to get up at six a.m.
  to water it

      **AMANI** *rolls her eyes, she's not actually*
      *mad though. she smiles a little too.*

  but she loved you more than she loved
  anything
  and she made me promise her when you were born

  that we'd / find a way to give you the universe

**DASIA.**  / find a way to give her the universe

**SMITH.**  dasia was five feet and five inches tall[1]
and she could have would have
found a way to
stop a train
going at the speed of light
for what was right in the world.

**AMANI.**  like she would have stood in front

**SMITH & DASIA.**  nah

**SMITH.**  dasia would have found some way

but i don't think she would have stood in front
she loved herself too much to stand in front
she knew the power of her voice too much
to go to death unless that was the only way
and she would have known
that's never the only way
she would have talked to the powers that be
she would have talked to god
and the angels
and the elements
the wind and all that shit
she would have conversed
with the cosmos
and stirred up a war
and took to the streets
and built up an army
but i think she would have thought
to her self

---

1 the actor playing **DASIA** can be any height in the spirit/ancestral plane

**DASIA.**  'what good it gonna do
       if i am dead?'

**SMITH.**  so she would have demanded her peace
       her rest
       in the fighting too.
       but she would have found some way

               *beat*

**AMANI.**  and how y'all meet

**SMITH.**  maniiiiiiii

**AMANI.**  daaaaaaaad

**SMITH.**  iwsskating

**AMANI.**  you were what

**SMITH.**  *(laughing)* mani

**AMANI.**  daaad

**SMITH.**  i was roller skating down this street
       and i saw your ma standing
       on this porch
       drinking a glass of lemonade

       i had passed this house every day
       but i never noticed
       how bright the yellow was

       and maybe it was the yellow of the lemonade
       and the yellow of her dress
       against the yellow of this house
       that made it all so bright.

       i didn't see that tree there
       till it was too late

i had these big glasses back then
these coke bottle glasses
and they shattered into a trillion pieces
and i couldn't see for shit without 'em

but i heard your ma
cracking up laughing
at this tall lanky boy sprawled out
at the end of her street

and i asked her if she could help me
and she led me to this porch

and she bandaged up my knees
and she rinsed off my skates
and the whole time she didn't stop
laughing and all i could really see
was yellow

**AMANI.**  that's my favorite story
you tell it different every time
last time you said she bandaged up your hands
and that your glasses shattered into a hundred pieces
not a trillion

> **SMITH** *stares at her for a moment*
> *what follows is of another plane*

**SMITH.**  how time goes. how GREAT this life is.

**DASIA.**  i want her to know from the bottom of her feet
that she is infinite.

**AMANI.**  dad

you think there is yellow paint on the moon?

when we get there i want to build a house
just like this one

**SMITH.**  i think there is yellow paint on the moon

    *beat*

**AMANI.**  they gonna kick us out.
that's what the sign means.
ms. davidson said
the word foras means
outside in latin
and those the same letters
as in F-O-R-/

**SMITH.**  /what your name

**AMANI.**  Amani

**SMITH.**  how you spell it

**AMANI.**  A-M-A-N-I

**SMITH.**  what it mean

**AMANI.**  dreams

**SMITH.**  and why that your name

**AMANI.**  cause i'm walking
with a million dreams
in stow

**SMITH.**  and what's the name of this house

**AMANI.**  Amani's House

**SMITH.**  what's the name of this ship

**AMANI.**  Amani's Ship

**SMITH.**  i said what's the name of this house
what's the name of this ship

**AMANI.**  AMANI'S HOUSE!
AMANI'S SHIP!

**SMITH.** so i don't care what no notice say
i don't care who steps through this door
claiming they got a right
to these walls
i don't care if i'm here or not here.

while you breathing
you better speak it.
this your house.
you own this.
you hear me?

**AMANI.** i hear you.

**SMITH.** until we get this to fly, this house is your inheritance
and i'll be damned if i let any motherfucker
with a sign come and fuck all that up.
*i will* stand in front of a train
going at the speed of light
for you
*i will*

   *beat*

but we gonna get this to fly
and we gonna go to the moon
and we'll build this house again
with yellow paint
on the moon.

when i was in that cage
i promised myself
that when i got out
i'd get you
somewhere
where there is no fear

when i got out
and saw the sun
as it shine here
i remembered every brick, rock and stone of this planet
is covered in somebody's fear
so we are going to the moon

and you will be safe
from every motherfucker
who would dare cross the path
to speak wrong to you
from the cops who stand
at the corner of charlemagne
from the work
that might take your body
from the fire
that's coming
and the water
that's coming
from the thought
that you are not enough
you will know you are enough
on the moon

you will speak as you speak
you will walk like you have a right to it
you will have a right to it
you will breathe easy
there will be no mirrors
except the water
and the water will hold you
and the water will hold me
and the water will hold

all them i left behind me
in that cage
they will get to hold themselves
again

**AMANI & SMITH.**  the water'll be blue everywhere.

**SMITH.**  and if you look in the water
you can see all the way down to the bed, you can count
the stones
that's how clear
everybody got a boat
we got a boat
with everything somebody need
to get through a day

**AMANI & SMITH.**  nothing more or less just breath

**SMITH.**  and god is god

**AMANI & SMITH.**  god like god in you and god in me

**SMITH.**  and sun ra is there
and he is playing ten instruments at once on the boat
across from ours
and i'm trying to figure out how in the hell that shit
don't sink
and sun ra see me looking
and he spend the rest of the afternoon teaching me all
at once
how to float and play and fly and there is no time

> *his mind has left the garden*
> *he has gone back*
> *many many years*
> *and forward*
> *many many years*

**AMANI** *brings him present*

**AMANI.**  dad

**SMITH.**  mani hey hey

**AMANI.**  you here

**SMITH.**  i'm here

**AMANI.**  okay

**SMITH.**  okay
measure this
on your own
you got it

## 2.5

## 2008–2010 & 1994//all time

**AMANI** *and* **KOFA**
*they are fourteen*
*and it is summer*

*mirror*
*breath*
*echo of our first image*
*energy*

*perhaps they, at the edge of childhood,*
*play their last hand game*
*something like rockin robin*
*body laughter breath*

*all at the same time,*
**DASIA** *sings in 1994:*

**DASIA.**  shades of delight cocoa hue
rich as the night afro blue

*she sit on the stoop, fireflies*
*she not waiting, just being*

**SMITH** *enters*
*through the gate*
*stops and looks at her for a long time*
*as if he is seeing her*
*for the very first time*

*she looks back*

*he doesn't say anything*
*there isn't anything to say*
*he sits next to her on the stoop*

*she leans on him*
*he plays with her hair.*
*her hair is thick.*
*the thickest thick*

*he knows how to*
*touch her hair*

*they breathe together*

*i been trying to find the words*
*for this scene*
*there are none*
*let it take*
*a long time*

**AMANI** *throws a note*
*folded into a paper airplane*
*to* **KOFA**
*but it lands before*
**DAVION** *who enters*
*like an eclipse*

# 3

# 2010

*the ship is recognizably*
*the beginnings of a ship*
*it's looking pretty good*
*for a ship made of wood*

**AMANI** *is fifteen.*

*it is before dawn, maybe four a.m.?*
*she creeps into the front yard*
*carrying a bookbag*
*something resembling a walk of shame*
*but she ain't all that ashamed*
*she thinks she is in love*
*who are we to say if she in love?*

*she is almost to the front door*
*she thinks she is in the clear*
*when* **SMITH** *emerges from the side of the house*
*with a two by four*
*he is preparing to cut*
*he has worked through the night and we can*
*see it*

*they stand off*
*there isn't really anything to say*
**SMITH** *would never hit his daughter*
*the thought of it*
*feels like a spirit*
*from somebody's plantation*

> *come to take over his hands*
> *he points to the hose*
> *she goes to the hose*
> *and waters the garden*
> *eyeing her father*
> *like 'you gonna give me my earful*
> *now or later'*
> *he eyes her back*
> *with a lot of fear*
> *masked as anger*
> *but we can see it*

**SMITH.** amani—

**AMANI.** i know i know
i'm sorry okay
just
he asked me to his prom

**SMITH.** you're not going to his prom

**AMANI.** he said he'd buy my dress and everything

**SMITH.** the hell he ain't
where he get money to buy your dress and everything

**AMANI.** he said he got it
so he got it
and i want to go

**SMITH.** i said you're not

**AMANI.** dad.

**SMITH.** that's the end of that

**AMANI.** daad—

**SMITH.** you are fifteen.

**AMANI.** so—

**SMITH.** /so he is too old!

**AMANI.** /it's two years!

**SMITH.** and i'll be damned
  if a motherfucker
  buys your dress
  with money from slinging
  i've worked too hard
  you're not going

**AMANI.** /he's not slinging dad
  not everybody is slinging

**SMITH.** /that's the end of it amani

**AMANI.** /what if you paid for the dress?

**SMITH.** it's not about the dress
  he is a senior
  his brain is on a different rhythm
  he's thinking about things you aren't ready for

**AMANI.** like whut

**SMITH.** like stuff you need to know yourself
  to be ready for

**AMANI.** what if i already did the stuff i'm not ready for

**SMITH.** amani

**AMANI.** i didn't
  i'm just saying what if i did

**SMITH.** where you been

**AMANI.** dad—

**SMITH**.  i said where you been

> *beat*

**AMANI**.  we went to the movies after school
and then we went to the park
and looked at the stars
it was cute
he's really cute
and really sweet dad
like i know you always say stuff
like don't let nobody treat you wrong
and blahblahblah
but i don't think he would
i don't think he could
like we laid out in the grass
and talked about constellations
and shit...stuff.
and he reached out and grabbed my hand
and he said

> **DAVION** *crosses to the edge of the garden*

**DAVION & AMANI**.  the very first second i saw you
in the cafeteria

**DAVION**.  i said to my boy
*watch* she gonna be mine

and so i wanna know
if you wanna go to prom with me
and i wanna know if you wanna
be my girl

> **DAVION** *exits*

**AMANI**.  and i felt like my stomach was falling to my knees
     and he kissed me.
     and i just lost track of time at the park
     i promise

          *beat*

**SMITH**.  that plant is dying

**AMANI**.  it's not

**SMITH**.  it is
     it's turning brown
     you ain't been watering
     you running around with boys
     who are too old for you
     and you forgetting what you got to do
     this is your garden

          *beat*

**AMANI**.  /i think i love him

**SMITH**.  /amani

**AMANI**.  just hear me out
     you were older than ma
     when y'all met
     two years right?
     it's the same thing.

**SMITH**.  /it's not the same thing

**AMANI**.  /it is

**SMITH**.  i said it's not
     and i said you're not going to prom
     with this boy who is seventeen

it's too old amani
and you talking about love?
you got to know yourself
to know something about love
you got to know what your
heart sounds like
and what your footstep
sounds like as it is different
from somebody else's footstep
you got to know what it means
to hold yourself
you can't even water your goddamn plants
you can't even care for this garden
and you talking about you in love
this boy held your hand
and asked you to be his
are you even your own
amani

**AMANI.**  of course i am my own
you taught me i am my own

**SMITH.**  well act like it

**AMANI.**  i am acting like it.
and i'm saying as my own
that i think i love him
and maybe i'm too young
to know what that means *exactly*
i don't know a lot of things.
but *i* can tell you i know what you meant
when you said all you could see was yellow

   **DASIA** *enters, sits and watches at the edge of*
   *the garden*

**SMITH**. amani...

   *beat*

 i want to meet him

**AMANI**. /so that means

**SMITH**. /i want to meet him
 that's what it means

**AMANI**. so i can go
 so i can say yes?
 i told him yes
 but that i gotta make sure
 it's okay but i can call him
 up and say yes?

**SMITH**. no. i said i want to meet him.
 that's what i said.
 that's all i said.

 if your plants start dying
 you can forget it
 not that i'm saying yes
 i'm saying you can forget
 the possibility

**AMANI**. okay

**SMITH**. okay

   *beat. a long silence.* **SMITH** *thinking, what if*
   *he hurts you?*

**AMANI**. i'll be alright dad

> **SMITH** *stares at her for a moment*
>
> *what follows is of another plane*

**SMITH.**  how time goes. how GREAT this life is.

**DASIA.**  i want her to know from the bottom of her feet
that she is infinite.

> *he hands her the two by four, she cuts, without
> help. they work for a while*

**AMANI.**  it looks good

**SMITH.**  i been working all night
while you been out galavanting

**AMANI.**  *(giggling)* "galavanting"
are you from like 1800?

> **SMITH** *chuckles too,*
>
> *a beat*
>
> **DAVION** *enters*

davion said

**AMANI & DAVION.**  there's no way
the ship will fly

**AMANI.**  he got the highest grade in the school
on the astronomy exam
and he said

**DAVION.**  i want to be a physicist
and i know there's no way the ship will fly

**SMITH.**  you ain't helping your case for prom

**AMANI.**  i ain't say nothing
ignore me.

*beat*

**SMITH.**  lotsa people gonna tell you this won't fly
but you got to believe what you believe
no matter what they say

**AMANI.**  gravity says otherwise
how i'm supposed to argue with gravity

**SMITH.**  lots of things people thought were impossible
happen all the time
and then they are not impossible anymore

remember when we thought we was gonna lose this house
and we found a way

**AMANI.**  nana caught us up on payments
from her shoe box savings
that's not a miracle
that's not an impossible
that's help dad

**SMITH.**  there is no difference
'tween help and miracle
we need each other
in this fucked up place

you and i
we put our hearts into this
we helping each other build, dream, make this
there is nothing that can stop us
there is no
impossible

**AMANI.**  davion say

**SMITH.**  you gone keep telling me what davion say

**AMANI.** some random boy i met on the sidewalk say

**DAVION.** in order for something to leave the orbit of gravity
    it'd have to be flying faster than the escape speed
    which is the amount of speed
    it takes for something to leave the gravitational orbit
    of another something

**AMANI.** and that random boy i met on the sidewalk say

**DAVION.** there's no way a nigga
    especially not a nigga
    from here
    could make
    something
    that
    fast

**SMITH.** you need to stop telling me shit
    about this dumb motherf—

**DASIA.** ask bout his heart

    *a beat,* **SMITH** *breathes*

**SMITH.** who are his parents?

**AMANI.** his mama white or real light or something
    and his daddy Black
    and they live on brooks lane

    *beat*

**SMITH.** don't believe nobody who tell you
    about the limit
    of your skin
    you hear me?

**AMANI**.  okay

**SMITH**.  okay

> *beat*

in three years' time
it will be ready
and we can go to the moon

> *beat*

**AMANI**.  will we come back?

**SMITH**.  /there won't be a need
we'll have everything there

**AMANI**.  /but if i'm in love

**SMITH**.  /we'll see when we finish mani/

**AMANI**.  /if i'm in love can he come

**SMITH**.  not if he don't believe
a person look like him
could make something
fast enough
he has no right
to the moon
he gonna have to figure out
where that comes from
and kill it
if he wants to go to the moon—

**AMANI**.  well i'll tell him
i'll start telling him
i'll help him figure out
what it is and help him kill it
so he can come with us

**SMITH**.  you can't help somebody
       kill something in themself.
       they got to want to kill it
       they got to kill it
       that's not your job mani

**AMANI**.  /i don't mind

**SMITH**.  /you can't run around killing other people's demons
       you gonna learn you got enough of your own
       you can't give yourself like that
       you'll wear yourself out like that

              *beat*

**AMANI**.  well
       i told him that i believe in it
       even if he doesn't
       and then we raced
       to the court
       and the streetlights were still on
       and somebody had left a ball
       and we played a game
       and i beat him
       in the race
       and in the game
       five–three
       and i said to him
       once i realized
       how late it was
       i said i got to go
       but see
       i am fast

and i
can
fly

   *and up comes the sun*

### 3.5

### 2011 & 1995//all time

**SMITH** *and* **DASIA**
**DASIA**'s *belly rise like magic*
*a baby grows from the garden*
**DASIA**'s *belly fall*
*and it is*
*1995*

*the sky is the bluest blue,* **AMANI** *coos*

*then*

**AMANI** *straightens her hair*
**KOFA** *paints their nails before the garden*
*they are sixteen. it is 2011*

*they help each other get ready for prom.*

*hold some time for alla them*

*mirror*
*echo*
*energy*
*no words*
*just*
*body laughter breath*

*before* **DAVION** *enters*
*like an eclipse*

# 4

## 2013

*just before dawn*

**AMANI** *watches a car speed away down the road*

*she holds a bouquet of roses and wears a dress for her prom*

*she wraps her arms around herself to try to hold herself*

*and the ship is done*

*and it is gleaming*

*at the edge of the garden*

**AMANI** *is eighteen and looks like her heart has been*

*pressed out of her chest*

*and she doesn't know what direction*

*is up anymore and what direction is down*

**SMITH** *emerges*

*from the backyard*

*in a suit he's made fit for the moon*

*he sees* **AMANI**

*and stops*

*a full and pregnant silence*

**AMANI.** all your talk of love and yellow

he gave me roses

you said

    a boy supposed
    to bring you roses
    so you know he a gentleman

    you said you brought my mama roses
    and she melted in your arms
    you said a boy supposed to make me feel like
    i am somebody

**SMITH.**  amani

**AMANI.**  i felt like i was somebody

                    **DAVION** *enters*

**DAVION.**  up there we ain't nobody

**AMANI.**  where?

**DAVION.**  college
    up there they make sure you know
    everyday
    you stupid

**AMANI.**  huh
    but
    i'm not stupid
    next year i'll go to college
    and they won't make me know
    nothing bout being stupid

**DAVION.**  yeah whatever
    you'll see
    you're just naive

**AMANI.**  naive?

**DAVION.**  you don't understand the world.

**AMANI.**  i understand i am full of light
i am capable of all things

i tried to tell him
he did not have to forget himself
to be

**SMITH.**  take off at dawn

**AMANI.**  i kept telling him and telling him
i tried to get him to kill it
the hate he's learned for all himself
and then
and then
he said

**DAVION.**  fuck!
you from nowhere
and
we grown now
and i got to find a girl
who
on
my
level!

i go
to a fancy school
far from here
and what is the moon
to a fancy school far from here
and i can't stay with a girl
with a crazy dad
who thinks he's gonna
go to space

there is no space
and you dumber than i thought
if you think
you gonna fly
and you dumber than i thought
if you think
i'm gonna
go with you

**AMANI**.  and he said all this
after we had
we had

and i didn't recognize him
anymore and i felt like
my body was splitting
in two
like i was watching
myself from outside myself
all at once
and he he he said

**DAVION**.  you hold yourself up
like god
pussy ain't no god

you too dark
so if you ever get to space
you will disappear

> **AMANI** *weeps*
> **SMITH** *pulls her to him and holds her*
> *his heart is breaking masked as anger*
> *but we can see it*

> *and then she breaks from him*
> *with rapid fire*
> *and all the anger she has for Davion*
> *transforms into anger for her father*

**AMANI.** make it fly!

**SMITH.** mani.

**AMANI.** i said make it fly!
you've filled me up with all these lies
all these stupid fucking lies

i am not great
i am not infinite

what is a dream
to a world like this?

make it fly!/

**SMITH.** not till dawn/

**AMANI.** now! let's go
let's leave this
planet
this ground
this earth
let's build this house
again on the moon
where he is not
where my mother can be
where i can be!
let's go
can we go?
let's go!

**SMITH**.  it will not fly till dawn
      you got to trust me
      it needs the light

**AMANI**.  fuck the light
      we got no light
      there is no light

**SMITH**.  amani!

*she is panicking*
*flipping*
*spinning*
*she runs her body towards the ship*
*and pummels it with her fists*
*and when her fists*
*are bloody*
*she finds a hammer*
*and breaks wood*
*splits wood*
*again and again and again*
*and* **SMITH** *is standing there*
*watching*
*and he is scared*
*not of her, but of this world*
*and he walks to her anyway*
*and grabs her in his arms*
*and they collapse together*
*on the bones of this broken ship*
*and they both weep*
*and there is suddenly enormous noise*
*and sirens*

> *and again she breaks from him*
> *and she stands as if she will strike*

**AMANI.** there is no space!
there. is. no. space!

> *and she runs away*
> *fast*

# ACT TWO



**AMANI** *is not a child anymore*

*the lights of a police car flash against* **SMITH**'s *face*
*a pulsing balance 'tween embodiment and text*
*all time conflates, crashes, bleeds, breathes*
*where violence is narrated*
*it is spoken with love in back of throat*
*this is not recounting*
*of numbers*
*this is*
*remembering*
*a human*

*a chorus, community*
*the*
*streets*
*remember*

**AMANI.**  /how many
men fulla shit
like my father

had me out here believing in the stars
talking bout the galaxies
in a ship made of wood

on the corners and edges
he's carved

**ALL EXCEPT DASIA.**  /dasia
dasia
dasia

**AMANI.**  /talkin bout ruling the world
shit
when i just wanted to be in it
how deeply i just wanted to be in it
to *be*
not excel
not extraordinary
but
just *be*
amani
shit
what kinda bullshit
to feed a Black girl bout
tomorrow where there no certain tomorrow
to talk bout the stars
like they close enough to touch
like she can fly if she want
she can take off
like she invincible
in an earth weighed down by gravity
inevitable
we coming down
and it's inevitable
i shoulda known
you know?

memories of my mother
rise up
like
'you shoulda known'

>    *the* **CHORUS**, *the people, hum*

**KOFA**.  /according to the streets
and witness reports
dasia was twenty-five in a

**DASIA**.  /bright
blue
skirt

**KOFA**.  /too short
for they hips

**ALL**.  /and dasia walked like

**DASIA**.  /love stuffed in pockets
and god in step

**LAMAR DAVIS**.  /what's good ma

**AMANI & KOFA**.  /lamar davis
donned crimson

**DASIA**.  /i float by
untethered
boundless
on sore feet
i float
boundless

**LAMAR DAVIS**.  /i said hi to you bitch
dumb bitch
can't you see

all this red
don't you know i got niggas
from here
to the pacific ocean who would fuck
you
up
in that
blue

**ALL EXCEPT LAMAR DAVIS.**  /maybe they said

**DASIA.**  /i got my people too
i walk with my people too

**AMANI.**  /maybe they were
silent?
witnesses dispute
cannot distinguish between
a dead hood Blackgirl's
voice and

**AMANI, DASIA & KOFA.**  /silence

**AMANI.**  /and his gun appeared faster
than she could count to two

and that blood against that blue

**ALL EXCEPT DASIA.**  /that
blood
'gainst
that
blue

**AMANI.**  /and the people say

**ALL EXCEPT DASIA.**  /the people say

**AMANI**.  /she didn't
    even
    flinch

**DASIA**.  /a lie.
    i was not
    that strong.
    we rarely
    without fear.
    i flinched.

**AMANI**.  /streets say the cops were looking
    but only looking as hard as cops look
    when a Blackgirl
    gets killed

    but the streets were looking too
    cause my ma had cousins
    and family who loved them real real heavy
    they say dasia was *everybody's* favorite

    say
    say she had a quick tongue

**KOFA**.  /with a smile to turn a storm

**DASIA**.  /from gray to rose gold

**SMITH & AMANI**.  /faster than the speed of light

**AMANI**.  it was three years past the murder
    and i guess grief don't ever really go anywhere
    when you lose someone who is your world?

    i guess that grief just roots itself right in the center of you

**SMITH & AMANI**.  collecting energy and getting old until it
    becomes a black hole

**KOFA**.  /all kids wanna believe in something
you ain't a fool for believing in something
the stars ain't myths
after all
they exist
after all

**AMANI**.  /so when my father saw lamar davis at the corner
of charlemagne and frontage
he say he just

**AMANI & SMITH**.  /came up out his own body
pulled over so fast

**DASIA**.  /pulled a hammer from the side of his hip
so fast

**SMITH**.  /and started running full force

**ALL EXCEPT SMITH**.  /with blood in his eyes

**SMITH**.  /all the yellow
i once knew
turned to bright
bright red

**AMANI**.  /and he didn't stop
until that man was

**DASIA & AMANI**.  /almost dead

**AMANI**.  /it was summer and i was five

i was not there
but the streets
remember

the **CHORUS**, *the people hum*

/something must have clicked or called him

**DASIA**.  /i clicked
   called from heaven
   held his arm back
   gave his vision back

**AMANI & SMITH**.  /cause he
   stood up
   saw that man unconscious

**AMANI**.  /and took off running to nana's house

**AMANI & SMITH**.  /where we hid out for three weeks till
   the police came

**AMANI**.  /and they gave him

**AMANI & SMITH**.  /six years for aggravated assault

**AMANI**.  /i don't know what it is bout men
   that always got them
   destroying worlds

   i remember my father and i
   had just begun to breathe again

**SMITH**.  /without looking for dasia
   in every corner

**AMANI**.  /it was summer and i was five
   and a motherless Black girl

   wasn't no hugs or warm things in nana's house
   i held my breath everywhere

**AMANI**.  /i learned how to leave my own body

**KOFA, AMANI & SMITH**.  /by imagining the stars

**DASIA**.  /andromeda
   antlia
   apus

    aquarius
    aquila
    ara
    aries

**AMANI.**  /but i'm not a girl no more

**ASOM 1.**  /uh
    alright

**KOFA.**  /just i knew you back when—

**AMANI.**  /i'm grown now
    i'm mature now—

**KOFA.**  /which means you
    don't believe in nothing
    'cept what they tell you
    to believe?

**AMANI.**  /—means i know the difference
    between a dream and a fact
    means i know the difference now
    between
    black and white
    means i know where i stand
    know myself
    now/

**ASOM 1.**  /hmm.

**KOFA.**  /and who are you?
    what do you believe in now

**DASIA.**  /that you grown?

**AMANI.**  /ain't no Black girl
    can live on the moon

ain't no air up there
to breathe

**DASIA.**  /your hair
dry
you have not
tended how can—

**AMANI.**  /i'm telling you all this
cause if you want
to meet my father

you gotta know

he will show you
the blueprints
for a rocketship made of wood he claims will fly

if you don't believe him
he'll say that when he finishes
he'll leave you here
in this fucked up city
to wait for the atomic bomb
or the end of the world
or whatever is coming

if you meet him
he will tell you how on the moon
there will be no cages long as he is king
my father claims he will be king of the moon
cause he will be the first to walk on it
my father swears that white man was a hologram
a fucking myth
he'll tell you that too

and i'm telling you all this
cause if you meet
my father
you have to be prepared

lotsa people
where i'm from
say he was not
sane, well, whole
lotsa
people where i'm from
don't know
how
to make sense
of him

**KOFA.**  /what do *you*
    believe in
    now?

**DASIA.**  /your hair
    dry you have not
    tended how can—

**AMANI.**  /he'll ask you to stand up tall and tell him
    all the things you believe in and all the things you are
    afraid of

    my father will tell you nobody
    who has lived more than a year in prison
    is afraid of what they are afraid of
    and he will ask you
    'what right you have to sit in fear of ghosts?'

**ASOM 1.** hmm

**AMANI.** so

> **ASOM 1** *sits up from where he is in Amani's bed*

> *beat*

**ASOM 1.** oh

**AMANI.** yeah

> *a series of men #1*

**ASOM 1.** thassa lot

> *beat*

i love you but
i'm sorry
i don't know if i love you enough
for all that
so i'll see you
bye

> *and he leaves real fast*
> *and this that follows should also be real real fast*
> *like an endless revolving door*

> *dis nigga a clown*
> *(i.e. this should all feel pretty absurd amidst the violence of toxic and performative masculinity)*

**DASIA.** /your hair is dry you—

> *a series of men #2*

**ASOM 2.** /hi.

**AMANI.** /hi.

**ASOM 2.** /i don't like
small talk

**AMANI.** /me neither

**ASOM 2.** /and
i saw you cross the room

**AMANI.** /i saw you too

**ASOM 2.** /and
let me just
cut to it

uhhhh

iwannafuckyou

**AMANI.** /ummm okay

**ASOM 2.** /so let's go

**AMANI.** /yeah okay

**ASOM 2.** /you like that

**AMANI.** /yup

**ASOM 2.** /you like that

**AMANI.** /unhuhh

**ASOM 2.** /you like that

**AMANI.** /for sure

**ASOM 2.** /you like that
you like that
you like that
you like that

**AMANI.**  /what?

**ASOM 2.**  /i said you like that

**AMANI.**  /oh
     sorry. i don't know what i felt
     what i'm feeling
     i don't remember the last time i was
     allowed to feel
     myself
     to know what i am feeling
     i—can you—
     can we—
     can you—
     can we—
     can you

     uhhhh
     have you ever heard
     *a love supreme*?

**ASOM 2.**  /ooooookay.
     i'mgonnago

**AMANI.**  /bye

**ASOM 2.**  /bye

**AMANI.**  /bye

**DASIA.**  /your hair dry you have not—

**ASOM 3.**  /hi
     have my babies

               *a series of men #3*

**AMANI.**  /oh. what.

**ASOM 3.**  /let's get married now
and have some babies
and you can move
with me
and i'll take care
of you
and it'll be forever
me and you
and you and i
and that'll be...
that'll be that
and i'll be man
and you'll be wife
and that'll be...

that'll be that

**AMANI.**  /can i be Man
and you be wife
what is Man?
are you Man?

**ASOM 3.**  /whuuut

**AMANI.**  /nothing didn't say nothing
sometimes i just say stuff
that doesn't make any sense
if that works...for you
for you...if that works.
uhhhh

**ASOM 3.**  /whut?

**AMANI.**  /you think
sun ra

went
to saturn?

**ASOM 3.**  /oh shiiiit
what if the condom broke

**AMANI.**  /don't fuck around like that

**ASOM 3.**  /*(laughing)* no like shit
like what if
it
accidentally
broke
and you
accidentally
have my babies

**AMANI.**  /can you stop fucking around like that

**ASOM 3.**  /i'm serious
like what would we name
it

**AMANI.**  /i'm tired

**DASIA.**  /your hair dry
you have not tended
how can—

**ASOM 4.**  /i'm here
i'm listening

*a series of men #4*

**AMANI.**  /you promise?
hold me.

**ASOM 4.**  /i'll hold you

**AMANI.**  /love me.

**ASOM 4.**  /i love you

**AMANI.**  /i'm scared

**ASOM 4.**  /we're all scared
  this is scary.

> *a very very long beat*

but i'm a MAN.

**AMANI.**  /Okayyyyy...
  /get offa me.

**ASOM 4.**  /i'm a MAN.

**AMANI.**  /get offa me.

**ASOM 4.**  /you love me?

**AMANI.**  /right now i just need—

**ASOM 4.**  /i'm a MAN.
  i'm a MAN.

**AMANI.**  /i need—

**ASOM 4.**  /i'm a MAN.

**AMANI.**  /what's a man?
  what you do with that?
  what you do with being a man?

**ASOM 4.**  /a Man provide
  a Man decide
  a Man fulla pride
  a Man get a bride.
  a Man ride
  a Man A Man a Man
  be my canvas?

**AMANI.**  /what?

**ASOM 4.**  /i am angry
at this world
let me write
that on you.

**AMANI.**  /i am angry too
i don't have room
for you to write—

**ASOM 4.**  *(he gestures writing)* I AM MAD. I AM A MAN.

**AMANI.**  —but i am already mad!

and there ain't no space for it.
are you listening?

i am already mad and there ain't no space for it!

i been mad.
all my life, a thousand years…

i been mad before you were mad.

where i write it?
where i write that i am mad?

somebody make a room

that is just
for
Blackgirls
to
scream.

 *and here a whisper*

/you cannot write your mad on me.

**ASOM 4.**  /there i'm done.

**AMANI.**  /you're done.

**ASOM 4.**  /let me hold you
    i am listening.
    i am listening now.

**AMANI.**  /were you listening then

**ASOM 4.**  /i don't listen when i fck

**AMANI.**  /oh.

**ASOM 4.**  /i can't listen when i fck
    if i listened i wouldn't be able to fck.

**AMANI.**  /oh.
    i am tired.
    can you get offa me
    for five minutes

**ASOM 4.**  /lemme hold you
    i am listening now

**AMANI.**  okay.
    i—

**ASOM 4.**  hey
    i'maman
    sorry fckkk it's like word vomit
    it's like a tic

**AMANI.**  clearly

**ASOM 4.**  but i'm listening

**AMANI.**  yeah?

**ASOM 4.**  forreal now

**AMANI.**  okay.

        *beat*

do you think sun ra
made it to saturn?

    *he thinks*

**ASOM 4**.  the calculable likelihood
of a Black boy born of birmingham
named after a magician
making it to saturn
with no space ship
and just a synthesizer
a buncha poems
piano hands
and a funky suit
and making it back alive...

real slim

saturn hot

the surface burns

it'd burn him up

and after all
if the aliens come
for somebody great
guarantee
they ain't checking for
no nigga from—

**AMANI**.  and me?

**ASOM 4**.  what, you?

**AMANI**.  you think i can
make it
to saturn
if not sun ra?

**ASOM 4**. uhhhhh

**AMANI**. you ever heard *a love supreme*?

**ASOM 4**. course
    classic
    coltrane—

**AMANI**. you think it's real?

**ASOM 4**. wht?

**AMANI**. a love supreme.

**ASOM 4**. of course it's real.
    coltrane had to know it
    couldn't have made
    it if he ain't know it
    like the back of his hand
    wouldn't have
    held up
    woulda sounded empty.

**AMANI**. think it's something
    that exists on earth
    or just between a MAN
    and his sax?

        *a very long beat*

**ASOM 4**. I don't know.
    Thassa lot
    I gotta go.
    But I love you, okay?
    You are mine, okay?
    I'll be back, okay?

**AMANI**. you said that last time—

**ASOM 4**.  when I need you again,
I'll be back.
Promise.

**AMANI**.  what if i need—

> *a door slams somewhere in the universe*
> **ASOM 4** *is gone as quickly as he appeared*
> **AMANI** *in front of a full length mirror*
> *somewhere in the universe a clock ticks*
> *a thousand years*
> *a million years*
> *she cries*
> *contorts*
> *hyperventilates*
> *breaks*
> *cannot figure out how to exist in her own body*
> *she picks herself apart*
> *until she is just bones*
> *she imagines the fat falling off her body*
> *till she is just bones*
> *the world caves in*
> *the world caves out*
> *her hands burn*
> *she shatters the mirror*
> *he does not come*
> *she cries again*
> *again*
> *again*
>
> *a sharp pain on her left side*
> *sends her reeling*

*in this dance
she screams*

*and in the
sonic cadence
of this scream...*

## Healing Movement 1

**DASIA**.  checking air pressure valves: thin
checking engine power, soil: dahlias overgrown 'n
weeds
checking light: approaching dawn
limbs, ready?:
nah heavy
wit self-hate
checking heart?: grief's
gaping wounds
hair? fuck. so dry.
checking feet neck belly flesh
checking...ready? we ready? dawn comin
need the light

**AMANI**.  fuck the light

**DASIA**.  checking tongue? watch your mouth
i am
your mother.

**AMANI**.  mama?

**DASIA**.  checking tongue. language
mind known?
heart known. ready?

**AMANI**.  mama?

**DASIA**.  are. you. ready?

dawn coming light dawning
and everything gone dry

**AMANI**.  i don't understand—i—

**DASIA**.  have shed most my english
no need here

most things require no language
retain few words
few songs for speaking to the living

so bear with me.
got to listen.

your hair
dry you have not tended
how can your garden grow?

how can your ship fly
with no
water
all flesh
and breath need water
it's how
we know we kin

breathe with me and imagine

**AMANI**.  mama i can't—

**DASIA**.  breathe
with me and
imagine

> **DASIA** *invites* **AMANI** *to sit before her*
> *in order to twist her hair*
> *she hands her a spray bottle*
> *full of water*
> **DASIA** *twists*

what are

the colors in
*your outer space?*

        **AMANI** *closes her eyes*
        *she imagines with her body, lots of breath*
        *and true discovery*

**AMANI.**  it's just
green mama
everything
everywhere
green

        **ASOM 4** *enters with roses*

and he's not
there
mama

but some part of me
keeps on asking

what if he comes back
and i'm no longer waiting

**DASIA.**  keep your tongue
bout you.

we two

spirit, body
a myth we control
any other thing
with breath.

**AMANI.**  i will not be here when he comes back

        **DASIA** *expels him out*

> *then **AMANI** opens her eyes*
> *a realization:*

**AMANI.**  he's not in my outer space

**DASIA.**  tend heart
twist hair everything gone dry
how can you fly
when everything
gone dry?

> **AMANI** *does not wrap her hair*
>
> *she sleeps*
>
> *time shifts; a click*

## Healing Movement 2

**DASIA.**  checking propellant
oxygen levels
breath

   *inhale*
   *exhale*

checking rest
center of pressure
focus
soil
checking heart, center, gravity
body: love growing up in the water
checking hair. fuck. still real dry
checking tongue language heart
tongue language heart
tongue

what words you got
what spells
to launch?

only the poem you write bout you
can heal you
nobody can build your ship but you

**AMANI.**  mama—
i don't have language

all these words
got no space for me
feel like i was a girl
and suddenly a woman

and was no room
for me to imagine the space between

**DASIA.**  had none for me neither
have always
just been *myself*

they got all these prisons
that could never know my name

pastors and porch ladies
talk bout my body before i got a chance to say
who dasia be
what dasia dream

but can't
erase me
their boxes not my death

for
somewhere i am living.

when i was living like you living
i sought to be whole
to stretch every finger
touch stars
take
space
where there
was no space
sought simply breath
sought simply home
in my own flesh

in the after life

i am all things

infinite

mm

got few words
for describing
afterlife
'cept
*free*
will not try
in this broken
boring
english

here to talk about
earth
here for you
before i rest

so

**AMANI.**  mama can i be all things?

**DASIA.**  baby you must
imagine your own space
between

so
oil and a scarf
to keep the water in

**AMANI.**  no one taught me bout my hair

**DASIA.**  can't hold it in
anger eat you up
what of you?
ain't this your life?

AMANI.  everything of this place
        say this life bout weight
        i had to grow up fast

DASIA.  i know
        i seen
        got to grieve
        to heal

        that wound there on your heart side

AMANI.  here

DASIA.  feel it?

AMANI.  i feel it mama.

DASIA.  from losing me

        that wound there on your right side
        feel it?

AMANI.  i feel it mama

DASIA.  from them locking up your father

        got to heal it

AMANI.  can't you just heal me then
        if you a dream if you a god/
        can't you just make me whole again?

DASIA.  /un-uhhhhh.

                *hand to belly,*
                *hand to heart to indicate*
                *the difference between*
                *god and Dasia*

        ain't no god
        a guide maybe

got no answers
only questions
can only point out where to look
you got the work.
so

**AMANI.**  i want

**DASIA.**  *(with softness)* go 'head

**AMANI.**  in my outer space
i want
pictures upon pictures
of you and dad
when you were living
want them lined across
the sky

want me when i was small
when i was infinite

want pictures
to remember
want to weep
freely
fiercely
want
couches i can disappear into
want a salve
made of soft stars
that i can touch
and press to flesh
to make these wounds
whole
again

**AMANI** *tends their scalp with water*
*seals it in with oil*
*wraps it with a scarf*
*a day a week or two*
*a year?*

*time shifts, a click*

## Healing Movement 3

> **DASIA** *removes* **AMANI**'s *scarf*
> *and begins to undo* **AMANI**'s *flat twists*

**DASIA.** checking neck, lifted
checking
language: spacious, and inevitably
insufficient
checking air pressure approaching perfection
checking propellant—so much breath!
ready dawn coming
we ready?

**AMANI.** mama
can we wait

**DASIA.** mhm waiting

> *they wait*
> *they breathe*
> **AMANI** *has learned to listen*
> *to her own body*

**AMANI.** why'd you have to die?

**DASIA.** some man was mad.

> *beat*

**AMANI.** can you stay
with me?

**DASIA.** on your plane
i'm dead
baby
but *you* are living

at some point
my work
complete
inevitably
grief

that is the stakes of death
so

> *beat*

**AMANI.** it sounds lonely, mama
just me myself in endless field of green

is there a love that's free?

> *time shifts, a click*
> **KOFA** *enters*
> *they stare at each other*
> *for a moment*

**KOFA.** all kids wanna believe in something
you ain't a fool for believing in something
the stars ain't myths
after all
they exist
after all

**AMANI.** i'm not a girl no more

**KOFA.** okay

i just knew you back when—

**AMANI.** don't act like you
know me cause you knew
me then

**KOFA.**  i'm not i—

**AMANI.**  just because we
　　were friends growing up
　　don't mean you know me now
　　it's been a long time
　　since we were were sixteen

**KOFA.**  i know

　　okay

**AMANI.**  i'm grown now
　　i'm mature now

**KOFA.**  which means you
　　don't believe in nothing
　　'cept what they tell you
　　to believe?

**AMANI.**  means i know the difference
　　between a dream and a fact
　　means i know the difference now
　　between
　　black and white
　　means i know where i stand
　　know myself
　　now

**KOFA.**  hmm.
　　and who are you?

**AMANI.**  what?

**KOFA.**  what do you believe in now?
　　that you grown?

　　　　*beat*

**AMANI**.  ain't no Blackgirl
    can live
    on the moon
    ain't no air up there
    to breathe?

    i believe that

**KOFA**.  *(with charm, care, a deep love)*
    none here neither
    sky bout gray with smoke
    tv full with death

    yet we breathing

    plus that ain't what you believe

    that's what you don't believe

    what you believe, amani?

            *beat*

**AMANI**.  what you up to these days?

**KOFA**.  i'm getting my phd in astrophysics
    i wanna be an astronaut.
    one day i wanna go to outer space.

**AMANI**.  mama, i've never felt more seen

            *beat, some time, **AMANI** imagines*
            *with the body*
            *and finds...*

**DASIA**.  all need
    a witness

    keep naming
    what you need.

your tongue
power
words
bear
fruit

    *a ritual, keep going:*

so

**AMANI.**  on my ship

i need
food enough for a billion years
water too

      *with one hand*
      **DASIA**
      *writes*
      *upon the sky*

and ain't no rules
bout love or gender
on my ship
nor in my outer space
nothing to box me in
free from all conceptions
bout who i ought to be
free from all labels
seek to contain me

simply AMANI

i'll love the journey
much as the destination
mama

and across the belly
of my ship will
be stretched the words

*a love supreme*

mama
i will love big
and many
and without fear

i will not hide my tongue
my self
from those who cannot hold it
cannot hold me

mama
i want love
that loves itself too much
to stand in front of a train going at the speed of light

i want love that will talk to god
and the angels
and the elements
and the wind
converse with the cosmos
dream up some freedoms
call in some futures
conjure some storms
dance till we sweat sweet
take to the streets

i want love that will think to itself

I DESERVE TO LIVE!

*a whisper:*

cause

i deserve to live

mama


i want love that will demand its peace
its rest in the fighting too

i want
friends and lovers
people holding me up
on every single
side

love that will not forget me

love that does not lie

mama
our outer space got to have
some joy

i want
some yellow
mixed in with green
want laughter
bouncing off
the cosmos
want
dahlias
from our garden

mama
want
quiet

want stillness

want breath

mama

want

so

much

space

> *the twists are undone*
> *and the twistout immaculate*
>
> *and then in a language*
>
> *that is not ENGLISH*
>
> *and ideally not from Europe at all*
>
> *and perhaps just a collection of sounds that*
> *are from no-place which is every-place* **DASIA**
> *says*

**DASIA.**  all that
which
you name
echo 'gainst
universe
and bounce back
'pon
you

> *and* **AMANI** *looks*
> *in the mirror*
> *and sees*
> *herself*
> *as herself*

*for the first time*
*in a long time*
*and* **AMANI** *breathes*

# ACT THREE

## 1

## 2017

*and up comes the sun*
*and in the sun*
**KOFA** *stands*
*back to back with* **AMANI**
*for a while these two*
*search for each other in their respective worlds*
*they each must find some peace in the body*
*before they find each other*
*and then*
*once they do*
*their loving in its many forms*
*is mutual*
*reciprocal*
*abundant*

*all of this should be choreographed*
*with enormous specificity*
*enormous care*
*and tenderness*
*it should embody the playful spirit of the best*
*of friends*

*belly laughter and inside jokes*
*and the tender witnessing of lovers*

*this is how long*
*it takes to even start healing*
*to even remember*
*we can breathe;*

*make motherfuckers*
*wait*

*mid laughter*

*a living space*

**AMANI**.  remember ms. davidson's
screechy ass voice?

**KOFA**.  and how she could never pronounce my name?
yes
kah-fuh
kee-fuh
core-uh
like girl.

**AMANI**.  and that time she farted in class and tried
to play it off by yelling
at jerome yancey
for no reason at all

**KOFA**.  and that time she gave us detention
and we spent the whole time writing
bad poems
about fake deep shit

true shit

**AMANI.** like your mama and her coming to the states

**KOFA.** and your daddy and his ship

we thought we had it all sorted
the chaos

**AMANI.** you were the first person
to believe me

*beat*

**KOFA.** remember that time she caught you making
out in the hallway w davion

**AMANI.** aight you was sposed to be keeping watch!

**KOFA.** i wasn't keeping watch for you and that crusty
ass nigga

**AMANI.** kofa!

**KOFA.** amani!

*(some laughter, some lightness... a beat & a
breath)*

**AMANI.** /we fall out?

**KOFA.** /do you remember when?

**AMANI.** /no

**KOFA.** /me neither

**AMANI.** itwas just

one day
we were standing
shoulder to shoulder
and you were

**KOFA.** /weird as fuck

**AMANI**.  /so damn free

>   and i believed in the moon
>   and in the power of my father's dreams
>   and then the next
>   my breath was in my throat
>   and there was no air
>   and there were a thousand men
>   eclipsing the stars
>   on a planet i ain't recognize
>
>   that's what i remember
>
>   i missed you light years.

**KOFA**.  you were my first friend.

>   you forget about me?

**AMANI**.  never.

>   just
>   life took me somewhere
>   and here i am

**KOFA**.  here you are.

>       *beat*

**AMANI**.  tell me a bad poem

**KOFA**.  lol whut

**AMANI**.  like detention.

>   tell me a bad poem bout fake deep shit

**KOFA**.  true shit

**AMANI**.  yes.

**KOFA**.  okay.

> **KOFA** *goes to the aux and plays*
> *a jazz piece*
> *of five minutes[1]*

**AMANI.**  this ain't a poem

**KOFA.**  lol shuddup.

> *they laugh and listen*
> *we exist with them*
> *listening too*
> *before...*

**KOFA.**  like there have been nineteen Black astronauts who
have made it to space
five who were not men
all from america
ronald mcnair was
the only Black astronaut
aboard the challenger
which disintegrated nine miles
above the atlantic ocean
seventy-three seconds after lift off
seventy-three seconds he was in the air
seventy-three seconds he was free
and then
wind
dust
gone

---

[1] This moment is inspired by "Ron's Piece" by Jean Michel-Jarre A license
to produce *AMANI* does not include a performance license for "Ron's
Piece" or any third-party or copyrighted recordings. Licensees should
create their own.

he was like a really fucking good saxophonist

and he had brought his saxophone with him on the
rocketship

and he had planned to play a song

when he arrived and it would have been the first
original piece of music recorded

without the weight of earth

**AMANI.**  but he didn't make it?

seventy-three seconds and he—

**KOFA.**  above the atlantic ocean

and it's like

it feels like

something down

in the ocean

called him back

or some force of this planet

held him back

i often think bout ronald mcnair

and i'm like if this Black man could not make it with
his saxophone

if there is not a single Black person from beyond
america

how could i?

    *rest*

[lol] like

every halloween i was an astronaut

**AMANI.**  [lol] i remember

**KOFA.**  [lol] out a costume i made myself from cardboard
boxes

and cut up soda cans

i had read every single sun ra poem by the time i was
seventeen
i don't know if he went to saturn.
i still can't decide if he was just spouting off at the
mouth bout some dreams
or high as fuck on LSD.
i don't think it matters, really. i think what matters
is that this Blackboy from birmingham
believed he made it to outer space, believed the beings
there told him to quit school
and tell his story through music.
and he did that
he made experimental avant garde Black music
that was cosmic, eclectic and free
and it made me believe i could be myself as i was as i am
it made me believe that i could become an astrophysicist:
me, a weird only kid with a million questions swarming
'round in this single body
with a mother who had no time to know my heart and
keep the lights on
stumbling around with a cardboard box on my head on
the eve of november

*i* could make it to the moon

> *as* **KOFA** *speaks*
>
> *we see* **SMITH** *sweeping the garden*

and i'm writing my dissertation on the extraordinary
matter contained within black holes

we have no device with which to perceive them

even our *strongest* telescopes fall short
and so all we know of them
is born of their effect on other matter

inference
speculation
echo

i have been thinking a lot about
how my body
my face
my hair
matches
that of the suspect

creates a spinning
vortex
of terror

in this place
where they lack the tools
to know me

and so i learn
to hold
my breath

but

what if my existence
had absolutely
nothing to do with
them

what if
i knew
myself?

      *beat*

      *they rest in this*

i often am so in awe that this song exists in the midst of death

and i am *at once* like what the fuck am i supposed to do

on this strange planet and like well fuck i got to keep going anyway

and perhaps none of it makes any sense but i guess

if i got seventy-three seconds
i better breathe in it—

> *the three of them:*
> **AMANI, SMITH** *and* **KOFA**
> *inhale*

your turn

tell me a poem

true shit

## 2

## a return, a moment
## quiet

**AMANI** *enters the garden*
*and watches her father*
*the air buzzes*
*he has aged a thousand years*
*before the wreckage of the ship*
*he moves much older than a man of fifty*
*despite popular opinion*
*we age*
*and feel*
*and carry*
*and are very tender*

**AMANI** *picks up two pieces*
*of the shattered ship*
*and holds out her hands*
*to her father*

*an apology*

*an acknowledgement*

*an exhale*

*before...*

**SMITH** *exits*
*in the dark*
*and* **AMANI** *is left alone*

*this should feel like a blink*
*an instant*

*before **AMANI** gets dressed*

*in all black*

## 3

## a eulogy

**AMANI**.  my father

> he would have told you
> he's building
> a rocketship that's going to the moon
> where there will be no prisons
> to take away Blackboys' best years their dreams and
> things

> > **KOFA** *enters dressed in all black*

> my father
> he
> *would* have told you
> that nobody

> who has lived
> more than a year
> in prison
> is afraid
> of what they are afraid of
> and he *would*

> have asked you what right
> you have to sit in fear of ghosts

**KOFA**.  i would have said
> i'm afraid of
> falling out the sky on a rollercoaster
> and of falling out of a plane while it's flying

and of falling
in general
and of losing my tongue
and of losing my mind
i am afraid of the ocean sometimes
but sometimes i also
am in love with it
i am afraid of having Black children
in a world like this
i am afraid of driving
i am afraid of breathing
some days
and when i am with you
i am less afraid.
i am afraid of all of us
disappearing in this city
i am afraid of them
acting like we were never here
i am afraid of the rain
that's coming
and i am afraid of not
knowing you when it comes

can you *look* at me?

**AMANI.**  when i look at you
i think i'm already above
the laws of gravity

but i'm like fuck
there is a limit
and we are always approaching
that limit

and eventually we're going to hit that limit
and crash
and i don't know if i can handle that
when we crash
when we realize we are not infinite

**KOFA.**  i can't tell you if we'll crash or not
i can tell you that every day i'm grateful
to ask the question
to build again
to see you

i can tell you that when i look at you
i know we are above the laws of gravity
and we are under them too

we are both flying and right here

and right now
i'm here with you

as you grieve your father, okay?

**AMANI.**  okay.

> **AMANI** *exhales*
> *closes her eyes*
> *and hears the*
> *voice of her father:*

**SMITH.**  what's the name of this house?

**AMANI.**  *(a whisper)*
amani's house

**SMITH.**  what's the name of this ship?

**AMANI.**  *(a whisper)*
amani's ship

**SMITH.** i said what's the name of this house?

**AMANI.** *(a shout)*
amani's house!

**SMITH.** i said what's the name of this ship?

**AMANI.** amani's ship!—

>*this embodies infinity*
>*let them take space and time*
>
>*before*
>
>**KOFA** *has found some blueprints*
>*crumpled up in the weeds*
>*and brings* **AMANI** *present*

**KOFA.** amani—

**AMANI.** mhm?

**KOFA.** *(indicating the blueprints)*
i think
it would have flown

## 4

## 2023, an epilogue

**KOFA** *and* **AMANI** *in the garden*
*in suits they made fit for the moon*
*there is a ship.*
*might this work?*
*great enormous wings*
*each of which has stretching across*
*the words*
*[a love supreme]*
*an engine purrs*
*it waits*
*it is ready*
*they are ready*
*the house is also*
*a brighter yellow than we've ever seen it*
*it shines*
*anything broken has been fixed*
*it is home*
*home is nowhere*
*and everywhere*
**AMANI** *is twenty-seven.*
**KOFA** *is twenty-seven.*

**KOFA.**  dream of a land
   my soul is from
   i hear a hand
   stroke on a drum

**KOFA & AMANI.**  elegant me
    beautiful you
    dancing towards free-
    dom's all we can do

**AMANI.**  two young lovers
    face to face
    with undulating grace
    they gently sway
    then slip away
    to some secluded place

**KOFA.**  whispering trees
    echo their sighs
    passionate pleas
    tender replies

**AMANI & KOFA.**  lovers in flight
    upward they glide
    burst at the height
    slowly subside

**AMANI.**  and my slumbering fantasy
    assumes reality
    until it seems it's not a dream

        **DASIA** *and* **SMITH** *appear in the garden as if
        from air*

**DASIA.**  until it seems it's not a dream

**KOFA.**  until it seems it's not a dream

**AMANI & KOFA.**  for two for you and me

        *beat*

**DASIA & AMANI.**  shades of delight
 cocoa hue

**SMITH.**  rich as the night

**AMANI, KOFA, DASIA & SMITH.**  afro blue

   *and up comes the sun*
   *and off they go into the universe*

## End of Play

www.ingramcontent.com/pod-product-compliance
Lightning Source LLC
Chambersburg PA
CBHW070622120726
47909CB00004B/1284